Short Stories
Found Online

Short Stories

Found Online

by

Jonathan Day

*To Sarah,
With Best Wishes
From "Jonathan"*

DODO BOOKS

Copyright © Jonathan Day
& Dodo Books 2016

First edition Dodo Books 2016

This is a work of fiction
and any resemblance to persons
living or dead is purely coincidental.

The author asserts the moral right to be
identified as the author of this work.

ISBN 978 1 906442 42 2

All rights reserved.
No part of this publication may be
reproduced, stored in a retrieval system, or
transmitted, in any form or by any means,
electronic, mechanical, photocopying,
recording or otherwise, without the prior
permission of the publisher, nor be
otherwise circulated in any form of binding
or cover other than that in which it is
published and without a similar condition
being imposed on the subsequent purchaser.

Stories

Angel for Hire
page 1
2,200 words

Body Balloon
page 11
1,200 words

Green Fairy and Small God
page 17
7,000 words

Print Out Your Pet
page 50
700 words

Modesty Wear
page 54
1,700 words

The Cult of the Cosmic Egg
page 62
1,500 words

Bodkin's Bazaar
page 73
1,500 words

Live Your Dream
page 80
1,700 words

Breath of Nature
page 88
1,500 words

Callaloo
page 95
1,700 words

Angel for Hire

The bruise had started to fade.

Explaining it to other people meant lying, because admitting how it had been caused was too shaming. At least Sophie could now visit the hairdresser to have her roots touched up without the awkward chit-chat about everything bar the embarrassing elephant in the room. She only became blonde because He insisted. Refusing would have meant yet another confrontation in which she always came off worse.

Time to go online and see if eBay listed that football strip He wanted. It was impossible without the name of the club, which she had forgotten given all the other things on her mind. She only remembered that an angel had been in its logo. How could Sophie, a woman who loathed football, be expected to find the exact shirt from all the pages available?

A thumbnail for Angels' something-or-other popped up. Right colour, but on a Ken doll. So in frustration Sophie clicked on all the other angel links. They advertised everything from dodgy software to a book about Los Angeles' law enforcement.

Then an unexpected item caught her eye.

*** Guardian Angel***
Allow us to solve the problem of your dangerously demanding child.

Sophie often surreptitiously went online to see how other mothers coped and read articles offering advice, but had never come across anything like this before. And then there was the *"cost -* **Very Modest***"* in bold print, and then only payable for a successful resolution. Surely there had to be a catch - there always was.

But Sophie was desperate.

Should she, shouldn't she? What if He found out? Fortunately He only used his own computer. Her laptop was far too slow for online gaming. If only He had been a little better at them she might not have needed to put in so much overtime to pay the bills that were ratcheted up.

Some extraordinary scams found their way onto eBay, so she checked the Guardian Angel's rating. It was a 100% with many appreciative comments, some almost incoherent with relief.

Sophie clicked the angel wings icon over the large, friendly face of a Staffie terrier, which opened the link to the terms and conditions:-.

Services are only for those in genuine need.

A brief summary of the problem is required with application.

Well that was easy enough.

Sophie typed in the message box, 'A growing, greedy son with a violent temper when unable to get his own way.'

She filled in her name, address and secret email -

no phone number, just in case the monster boy answered it - then clicked send. In her heart she knew that this was an exercise in futility, yet doing it made her feel a little better. And if it was a ploy to sell something else, she couldn't afford it anyway. It was as much a she could do to pay off the interest on the loans needed to keep her son happy.

That brief moment of relief faded as she pulled on her coat to leave for the evening shift. He was up in his room, probably leaving malicious messages on Facebook pages users had dedicated to deceased friends and family members. So Sophie silently left, pulling the front door to without a sound.

By the time she returned at midnight, the fridge had been raided and a chilled six-pack consumed. He was now snoring on his bed. At least she and the neighbours would get some sleep that night. Sophie could have popped into His bedroom and removed the speakers as a precaution, but that would have only triggered a violent tantrum the next morning. It was too soon after the last assault to provoke another, so she went to bed.

The morning shift did not start until ten, so Sophie waited until eight o'clock before getting up and going down to the kitchen. He didn't usually demand breakfast until she was about to dash for a bus anyway and there was no movement from upstairs. Perhaps He had wandered out in the night, drunk, and fallen under a taxi? She should have been so lucky! Sophie scolded herself for thinking such a thing. He may have been a monster and destroyed her marriage as well as peace of mind, but He was her son after all. Wasn't that why she put up with all the aggravation?

She made a coffee, which was half way to her lips when there was a knock at the front door. The electric meter had only just been read and it was too early for the post to deliver yet another expensive electronic toy.

Mug in hand, Sophie padded out to the narrow hallway see who it was.

Standing on the pavement was a scruffy man accompanied by a Staffie terrier with a smiley expression.

'Sorry love,' she said, 'Can't spare anything I'm afraid. Everything I make is spoken for before it leaves the pay packet.'

Behind the beard appeared a genial smile that disconcertingly resembled that of the man's dog. 'I know, madam. It is I who have come to help you.' He handed her his card. On it were the angel's wings and smiley dog logo.

Now what should Sophie do? Invite the man in and risk her son descending on them like an enraged demon, or leave him chatting on the doorstep to give the neighbours yet something else to gossip about? God only knew that they were entitled to do that.

She made a snap decision. 'Come in.'

The tramp and his dog followed her into the kitchen where she made another coffee. 'Sit down. Dog like some water?'

'He only drinks lemonade.'

'Got some somewhere.' Sophie pulled out a half-empty bottle from a cupboard. 'Must be flat by now.'

'He won't mind.'

The dog enthusiastically lapped up the lemonade from the basin she placed on the floor.
Sophie sat at the table facing the visitor. His eyes were a startling blue, yet his skin - that which was visible under his tangled beard and unkempt hair - an amber gold.

'I really hope this isn't a joke,' Sophie whispered. 'I'm too near the edge, and a con like this just might tip me over.'

'I appreciate that. How long has your child been a problem?'

'Since he was born. We thought the boy would grow out of it. Been seen by the best specialists. They couldn't find anything to account for the way he carries on. We never spoiled him. When he was seven he knifed his young sister over a toy, so they took the poor little kid away for her own safety. Only manage to slip away and see her now and then. If he knew he would get jealous and probably knife me as well - not that he hasn't tried. He's just too old for me to manage any more. He was a nightmare before – now it's hell! Broke up our marriage, he did...'

Sophie started to become tearful.

'Please rest assured that my services encompass problems of this nature.' The dishevelled visitor seemed totally confident in his claim.

'I don't see how. Everyone has tried. Because there's nothing wrong with him, he would need to maim or kill me before the police intervened.' The tears were now flooding down Sophie's cheeks. 'How did this happen? I'm not a bad mother... My daughter's a lovely girl...'

'You are a generous and worthy woman inflicted with an aberration that could have been born to anyone. Had your child been disabled I have no doubt that you and your husband would have lovingly tended to his needs, whatever the cost. But there is no reward for nurturing a creature you cannot love, however hard you might try.'

There was no point in wishing herself back to those unenlightened times, so Sophie choked back the tears with the help from a mouthful of coffee. 'I don't mean to be rude, but what could you do about it?'

'Life has the most unexpected way of balancing things out.'

'I've lost a beautiful daughter. Even if he wasn't here, I could never take her back now. She's too happy with the family that adopted her and I would never do that. And even if you can do something, how do I pay you?'

'In the way you least expect.'

Sophie raised her eyebrows and backed away slightly.

'Nothing salacious or illegal, I assure you.' The visitor finished his coffee. 'Now, about your son.'

Something occurred to Sophie. 'That's odd. He would normally be down here like a shot as soon as he heard voices, hangover or not.'

The visitor's mouth formed a knowing 'Ah.' He had obviously anticipated that.

Sophie could tell that this "angel" knew more than he would admit. 'Just what is my son?'

He smiled sympathetically. 'Just a mishap, a very unfortunate mishap.'

'But he's my son...'
'Genetically maybe. Unfortunately some personalities can slip through into identities never intended for them.'

Sophie could barely grasp what he was saying. 'But he's not the only one like it. There are so many there's even a support group. I daren't join it in case he found out.'

'Owing to the increasing numbers, filtering their allocation has become a problem lately. Thank goodness for the Internet.'

His mystifying words took on a watery quality as Sophie unaccountably found herself dozing off.

When she woke it was still half past eight.

She had fallen asleep, head resting on the

kitchen table next to her mug of coffee. After being exhausted by all the stress, was she now starting to hallucinate, or could that visitor and his dog have been real? If so, they must have wound back the hands of the kitchen clock. And yet there was that basin on the floor licked clean of lemonade and other mug on the table. Then she noticed the card with the smiley dog and angel wings beside it. On its reverse was a note, "Thank you for the excellent coffee. Payment received and matter now dealt with."

Sophie tucked it in her dressing gown pocket and quickly rinsed out the visitor's mug before He came down.

Still disorientated, she made another coffee and went into the living room to rest in an armchair.

Eventually her thoughts cleared and she became aware of the changes. Her ghastly son was no longer in the photo taken with her husband when the boy had been an infant. The chair by the door where He always dumped washing was empty. All the discarded electronic toys, footballs and folder of Nazi insignia from which He was selecting a tattoo, had also disappeared.

Sophie rose, half hopeful, half fearful, and padded up the stairs to her son's bedroom. There was no skull and crossbones "keep out" sign on the door. She warily nudged it open and peered in.

The computer, sound system, horrific posters and Coke stains on the wall were all gone. The room was exactly as it was before becoming his; light, airy with faded flower wallpaper and lacy net curtains fluttering in the breeze from the half open sash window. And - best of all - He wasn't there!

Sophie wanted to burst into tears - of relief. No guilt, no regret, just relief.

It wasn't possible to wind back the years He had robbed her of, but at least she had her life back. Perhaps every record of her son had also disappeared from the files of the agencies called in to help her. If not, she could always tell them that He had left to join some right wing commune. They would believe that.

After a shower, another cup of coffee, and a phone call to say that she wouldn't be in to work that day, Sophie sat at the kitchen table deep in thought.

There was a knock at the front door.

Perhaps the devil offspring had changed his mind and come back?

Perhaps the angel had returned to demand real payment.

At that moment Sophie would have handed over her life's savings if she had any. She pulled herself together and went to answer it. Standing on the pavement was no tramp and his dog, or her ghastly son.

It was the husband who had left ten years ago.
'Ben?'

He looked sheepish. 'I've come to say sorry

Sophie. I should never have bailed out like that, but you know I would have killed that little sod if I'd stayed.'

Sophie had wished so many times that he had.

'He's disappeared from all your photos, hasn't he?'

Ben looked startled. 'How did you know?'

Then she noticed the five-year-old clinging to his trouser leg. She was a pretty, slight thing with huge hazel eyes. 'Who's this then?'

'Hamida. Her mother's...' He hesitated.

'How?'

'Honour killing for shacking up with me ... three years ago,' Ben whispered.

'Oh Ben ... I'm so sorry.'

Sophie didn't know what else to say.

As the angel had said, 'Life has the most unexpected way of balancing things out.'

Not only had she been relieved of a nightmarish son, but was being compensated with a beautiful daughter to cherish.

'Come inside Hamida. I'm making breakfast. Do you like scrambled eggs on toast?'

Body Balloon

It was blue - though also came in red, yellow or pink, depending on how you viewed the world you made such laborious progress through. Blue was the colour least likely to emphasise its size and, more importantly, the customer's size.

The Body Balloon came with options to support the "average overweight" to "unable to get up from a chair without assistance".

Herbert fell into the last category. He could never work out why, especially after cutting out fizzy drinks and junk food, and even attempting to peddle the exercise bike he purchased from the same company until it buckled. It shouldn't have done; being designed for users of a certain size, unlike workout equipment for the physically active, which made the assumption that their users were fit and mobile.

The doctor had fobbed Herbert off with platitudes about fluid retention and 'Why not try substituting fruit for chips or a hamburger,' sooner than saying, 'What? You on a diet? Pull the other one.' There was no point in trying to remonstrate. The medical profession was developing zero tolerance towards people they perceived to be victims of their own weakness. Yet, without them believing you, what hope had anyone of finding out why their waistline was expanding when they were not consuming enough to account for it?

So Herbert gave in, opened his online account and bought a bright blue Body Balloon, the newest innovation to replace the ubiquitous mobility scooter, which could be dangerous, unstable, and only emphasise the fact that you were so overweight you couldn't walk anywhere. The Body Balloon was not only bright blue, but fun, totally stable and saved both rider and pedestrians from dangerous collisions.

It arrived next day in a box containing the instructions, an air pump, charging unit, sturdy frame to which were attached several fans, a motor and battery. Neatly folded on top of that was what looked like a deflated dinghy.

After his breakfast of one slice of toast and cup of tea, Herbert dragged the box out into the small garden of his ground floor flat and assembled it according to the instructions.

When the Body Balloon was inflated he sat in the armchair shaped dirigible and gingerly switched on the motor, fully expecting it to collapse under his weight.

But it didn't. The fans levitated him a few inches from the ground so the chair could be turned in any direction with the slightest motion.

This could become very addictive. Herbert would attract attention of course, but surely only from people who wanted to know where they could get one.

Herbert manoeuvred the Body Balloon through

the side gate and found himself sailing along the pavement like potentate on a magic carpet.

People did stare.

Many of his neighbours had assumed Herbert to be housebound, no doubt disapproving of somebody barely out of their twenties being too overweight to work. Yet he was beyond embarrassment, knowing that the fault was not his, but that of the medical profession who refused to listen and diagnose what was actually wrong with him.

When it became apparent that the astounded expressions were not reflecting envy, but confused annoyance at the contraption taking up so much of the pavement, Herbert floated into the local park which was usually empty at that time of day apart from the occasional dog walker. Goodness only knew what small children leaving kindergarten would have made of his bright blue Body Balloon as it approached. Parents would have no doubt hustled them away with dire warnings against wanting one. All the same, he kept to the herbaceous borders for fear of being accosted on his maiden voyage.

Just as Herbert began to accept that this may be the mode of transport for the rest of his life and something to be enjoyed, the Body Balloon wobbled a little. He leant back to slow it down and take cover by a stand of philadelphus. Its perfume seemed overpowering enough to buoy him up higher. Herbert dismissed the ridiculous idea, and then realised that he was definitely going up.

Nothing in the instructions covered this eventuality. The buoyancy of the Body Balloon should have been strictly controlled so it could not rise any higher than six inches from the ground.

The instructions were wrong.

Soon Herbert's hair was touching the highest branches of mock orange blossom. Then, to his horror, he realised that he was being slewed sideways towards the huge, unpruned tangle of rose bushes. Many comments had been made about the viciousness of their thorns. The gardeners had planted them to deter children making dens in the border where they could secretly light fires, or drug addicts using its cover to shoot up.

Herbert tried not to panic and gently attempted to bounce the Body Balloon back to the ground. Unfortunately this made it more unstable.

He was now directly over the rose bushes.

This was embarrassing as well as scary. What would happen if the infernal device tipped him out? He would be left sprawling on the ground until some passer-by was obliged to call for help to get him up. No, not again, Herbert thought. The idea was too demeaning. So he tried to nudge the bright blue blob away from the brambles. But it refused to budge.

Then the inevitable happened.

After one last, desperate nudge the Body Balloon turned turtle, tipping Herbert into the thicket of rose bushes.

The Body Balloon was punctured by the vicious thorns, yet refused to deflate.

Herbert fared far worse. Stabbed multiple times by the ferocious barbs, he had no choice but to roll through the brambles to escape. He lay on the grass, panting, mortified with embarrassment, and lacerated.

Herbert glowered angrily at the bright blue Body Balloon hanging innocently above his head. There was no point in wishing it would deflate. He had to get back home somehow.

At least no one else had witnessed the mishap.

He managed to push himself up into a sitting position and, as the pain became more bearable, he realised that it was easier to move.

In fact, Herbert actually managed to stand up unaided for the first time in years.

Then his trousers fell down.

His waistline was rapidly receding. All the rolls of fat that had been the bane of his young life were deflating like a balloon. He looked down in amazement to see the pounds evaporating from him like melting snow.

Even more peculiar, the skin that had been stretched to contain his huge circumference retained its elasticity. Now Herbert was just a young man in ridiculously oversized clothes.

Once he had recovered from the astonishment,

the next thing that occurred to him was bizarre. Would anybody recognize who he was? Some busybody was bound to complain to the council that he had a lodger.

But that hardly mattered now. Herbert could find a job, perhaps even a girlfriend, and make something of his life.

He glanced up at the blue Body Balloon and decided to leave it there to amuse the children and baffle adults.

Who could tell? Perhaps there was some previously undiscovered life form on earth that might like to nest in it.

Green Fairy and Small God

Nobody noticed him come in.

A small man in his early forties wearing a suit, high-collared shirt and pushed back trilby just appeared before the desk sergeant. He had to be the most unlikely copper to enter their station. No one had expected the detective inspector sent to deal with the murder of a local family member noted for raising dangerous mobs to be so slight a light breeze could have blown him away.

The huge PS Harris looked down at DI Dalton and marvelled that someone this diminutive had managed to survive an unarmed combat course even though his stiff, upright posture suggested military training. With those bright, alert eyes he should have been stargazing or restoring illuminated manuscripts. It didn't help that PC Wren looked up from the timesheets she was working on to see if the small man was wearing a wedding ring. Her powers of deduction were quite often hormonal.

DI Dalton was there because the influential family claiming that their eldest son had been murdered had insisted that the detective investigating the case be removed. At least one good thing would come out of this. PS Harris would no longer have to accompany DI Knowles to the Gauvins' massive mausoleum of a country seat.

DI Dalton's partner arrived an hour later straight from armed response duties. She was a totally different kettle of fish; a woman built like the Rock of Gibraltar that PS Harris could look straight in the unswerving gaze. PS Atkins, who was assigned to accompany DI Dalton everywhere, cut a splendidly intimidating figure in uniform and protective vest, conceivably a ploy to counteract her superior's puny appearance. Even the local drug pusher waiting his turn to be interviewed seemed impressed. Fortunately DI Dalton and PS Atkins weren't there to interfere with the local constabulary's handling of petty criminals and dispensers of strange substances. Wealth and influence counted in their small corner of the world and PS Harris, amongst many, was glad that the troublemaking, racist Gauvin heir had jumped off the roof. It was somehow fitting that his last meal should have been in Mr Kapoor's popular Curry Palace, though unfortunately it made the restaurateur a prime suspect for spiking the food. On the other hand, it meant that the local police would no longer need to contain the anti-immigration rallies Jonah Gauvin regularly raised about the county. PS Harris was known for his short fuse and limited tolerance (his furious frown could intimidate the most brazen teenager), but knew that herding hard-working, vegetable picking immigrants back across the Channel would make dinners for the larger man much more expensive.

PC Wren blamed the Internet for persuading gullible minds to follow the Gauvins' ideology, and few argued with her. The IT savvy constable had saved many officer hours by ferreting out snippets of online information more clumsy fingers failed to make the connections for. But at that moment she was interested in DI Dalton. He had been assigned from a large town with almost 200 thousand residents. Its police force had a dedicated cyber crime unit consulted by other regions because of its impressive record. (Perhaps she might apply for a transfer when PS Harris wasn't looking over her shoulder.)

PC Wren decided to take a look on Panoramia.

The photograph of a beautiful Hindu temple immediately appeared. It had been built in a leafy suburb of the town some 30 years previously. With it was a brief history and links to several articles. One posting caught her eye; "Police constable rescues family from fire." She clicked on it.

'Come and look at this, Sarge. According to this blogger, 20 years ago a young constable from DI Dalton's force saved an entire family from a house fire. "After escorting the adults who had been overcome by smoke from their blazing home, he wrapped his hands and head in wet towels then went back in to rescue the children trapped upstairs. He smashed a window and dropped them onto mattresses neighbours had piled up." He didn't make it out. Firefighters found him later.'

PS Harris came across and glanced over her shoulder. 'Is that where they buried him?'

'No Sarge, it's a Hindu temple. But look, it says here that it has a shrine to his memory.' The prospect of facing a dilemma like that chilled PC Wren. 'Think you could have done something like that, Sarge?'

'Me? Not bloody likely.'

'Me neither. Strange this didn't come up when I checked our archives.' She tapped in a news search. 'Nothing in the papers of the day either.'

'It was over 20 years ago. The dead don't hang around to remind the rest of the world of how brave they've been. And look, that article goes on to say the newbie was a foundling brought up by Barnardos, so there wouldn't have been a family to remember him either, apart from the one who keep his picture in their temple.'

PC Wren read on. '"Because he arrived at the orphanage with no identity, the temple gave him a new one and revere him as Maderu Verma". Nothing else about him.'

While the rest of the small station speculated over them, DI Dalton and PS Atkins were being briefed by about the death of the Gauvin's eldest son. It could have been accidental, but accusations by the father that the local Indian restaurant had spiked his food with a hallucinogenic drug could not be ignored. Fitzroy Gauvin insisted that this is what caused the heir to this pillar - albeit dangerously right leaning - of the landed gentry to step off the roof to touch the moon. But then, the head of this household was also convinced that his family had been cursed by Kali for the misdemeanours of an ancestor.

'The food served by the Curry Palace was thoroughly tested and other customers had experienced no symptoms, but Fitzroy Gauvin remained convinced that his son had been poisoned that very evening. If he had allowed an autopsy that would have proved it one way or the other and saved police time,' explained DI Knowles. 'The man is delusional and his politics dangerous to public order, but can't be ignored. Had me thrown off the case when I insisted on fingerprinting the family.'

DI Dalton smiled. 'You were aware he would do that of course?'

DI Knowles prickled in annoyance and limited his response to, 'This needs the application of a more ...'

But his counterpart knew why he was there. 'Devious?'

'Intellect. Just try to prove it was an accident, or even the curse of Kali punishing the family for purloining so much treasure during the Raj.' DI Knowles vengefully slapped down the thick case file on the desk before the other detective. 'Just make it go away. Idyllic backwaters such as ours have too many influential idiots to deal with when we should be concentrating on dogs worrying sheep and broken street lamps.'

DI Dalton flipped through the dossier. 'Do you have anything relating to the Gauvin estate's finances?'

DI Knowles didn't see the relevance. 'That family keep things close to their chest. No one really knows what they're worth. Asking something like that would have really been pushing it.'

'Oh dear. Hacking into accountants' databases can be so time-consuming.'

'I didn't hear you say that.'

'Ignore the boss's sense of humour, Sir. It can be a bit odd at times.'

The way PS Atkins said it made DI Knowles even more suspicious. He could see why the chief inspector insisted that this small man had a partner with him at all times. If anyone took exception to what he said there needed to be someone to pick him up.

Once out of earshot, PS Atkins turned to her superior and scolded, 'You can really push your luck at times, you know.'

'I know. Where have you parked our car?'

'Outside the hotel. It's only a two minute walk.'

'Good. You can take the forensic kit up to my room and lock it in the wardrobe while I find a quiet corner in a teashop with Wi-Fi so I can talk to my elves.'

DI Knowles expected to hear no more from them. Then PS Atkins was unexpectedly called away on urgent armed response unit duty. He was obliged to replace her and the car. There was only one other officer familiar enough with the case, and PS Harris was not happy at the prospect of wet nursing the gnat of a man.

'Me? Take orders from someone who never loosens his tie?'

'Do as you're told,' ordered DI Knowles. 'And don't turn into the Incredible Hulk when he gets annoying. And, whatever you do, don't let him out of your sight.'

'Isn't he allowed out on his own then?'

'Must have a uniformed officer with him at all times. One of the conditions we got him.'

PS Harris was still grumbling under his breath when he left PC Wren in charge of the front desk.

He found DI Dalton sitting in a corner of the Coffee Pot, busily tapping away at his laptop.

The detective showed little surprise that his sergeant had gone. 'She likes playing with guns. It's her hobby.'

The rustic chair creaked with the weight of PS Harris as he sat down opposite him. 'What's the routine, Sir?'

'Have a cup of tea. The Darjeeling is quite

decent.'

The waitress knew what the local constabulary preferred and brought him a hot chocolate.

At last DI Dalton looked up from the keyboard. 'Were you aware that the Gauvins have multiple offshore accounts squirrelled away in as many countries and own property in London, the Algarve and Cornwall?'

'Then why are they living out here in the back of beyond?'

DI Dalton ignored him. 'And are worth at least 60 million pounds? More than enough to fund their little forays into immigrant bashing. And Fitzroy Gauvin's will is certainly worth looking over.'

'I wouldn't have a clue how to hack into a solicitor's files.'

'Some firewalls can be quite daunting.' Then the detective realised that this was not polite interest. 'Your badly suppressed snarl suggests that you don't approve.'

'I would like to leave the force with a pension, if it's all the same to you, Sir.' A moustache of froth appeared on the large man's face as he swallowed his hot chocolate.

DI Dalton handed him a paper napkin. 'Perhaps if we pay the family a visit we might learn more.'

PS Harris doubted it. The Gauvins wouldn't tell you the time without a court order, but he relished his new boss finding that out for himself.

He had no idea why he allowed DI Dalton to drive them there in the unmarked car. The hacking of confidential records he could ignore because he was a dinosaur as far as technology was concerned, but collisions with unsuspecting trees was another matter and he confiscated the car keys as soon as they arrived at the palatial home of the landed gentry.

He pointed to a high, flat roof surrounded by a low railing. 'Eldest son jumped from up there.'

But the detective's attention was elsewhere and he crossed the courtyard to study the shrubs surrounding it. PS Harris refused to believe that this man had ever lifted a garden fork in earnest, so assumed there was something DI Knowles had missed during the initial investigation.

The DI was picking a couple of silver green leaves from a bush when the heavy oak door at the head of the sweeping steps opened. A stern looking butler and middle-aged man with distinguished features appeared. As DI Dalton placed the leaves inside his jacket a young man bounded excitedly from an outhouse adjoining the conservatory.

'You won't find any clues in those bushes, you know! Only dog poop! Daddy will let his puppies use it as a latrine. Really annoys the gardeners.'

DI Dalton turned to see one of those puppies being restrained by the butler. It was fixing its evil gaze on him.

PS Harris glowered at it and the Doberman drew back.

'This is DI Dalton, Sir. Come down especially to look into the case.' There was an edge to the policeman's tone as he added, 'As you requested.'

Fitzroy Gauvin let the underling's sarcasm pass. He was looking at DI Dalton in disbelief. From the other side of the courtyard the detective could have been taken for a 12-year-old if it hadn't been for the inflexible way he moved. At least the man had decent dress sense, unlike the dishevelled DI Knowles.

DI Dalton came over to hold up his police ID in case the landowner refused to believe it.

'Come inside,' Fitzroy Gauvin ordered and the butler escorted them through the hall to the large dining room.

'You didn't experience any digestive problems at the same time as Mr Jonah Gauvin, did you?' the DI asked him.

But Fitzroy Gauvin overheard and turned angrily. 'You don't question my staff without permission! Get out Cameron!'

The butler dipped a bow and discreetly left.

'See what I mean, Sir?' PS Harris whispered.

'You're snarling again.'

It was perversely gratifying to see how unflappable DI Dalton was as he impudently circled the spacious room in his oddly stiff gait, examining

Indian antiques. 'You have a remarkable collection here, Mr Gauvin.'

The head of the family turned his back to show his contempt of the DI's disrespectful manner.

'Oh yes,' Connor, the surviving son who had followed them in, chirped up. 'All purloined from a Mogul palace during the Raj.'

'Indeed?'

'One of our ancestors was something of an adventurer.'

DI Dalton briefly examined a bronze statuette of Ganesh. 'And a handler of counterfeit goods,' he muttered under his breath.

Fitzroy Gauvin caught the last part of his comment and turned back furiously. 'What did you say?!'

The detective tapped Ganesh on his broken tusk. 'His trunk turns the wrong way and this fellow's companion was a rat, not a monkey.'

'And what would you know about it?'

'I know that it is unlikely that such a large collection of Hindu gods would be displayed in a Mogul palace.' DI Dalton took an evasive route around Gauvin to reach the black ceramic statuette of Kali sitting in pride of place - somewhat unusually for an artefact that was the cause of the family's woes - by the marble mantelpiece. 'And I assume that this one is supposed to be responsible for the curse?'

Gauvin glowered uneasily as DI Dalton dared to lift it, his expression warning him to replace it on the stand immediately. The detective chose not to notice and closely examined Kali.

'All of these artefacts would have been returned years ago if we could find out where they came from of course,' Connor told him. 'Daddy believes that they have been draining the life from our family, although I blame Mr Kapoor's curries myself. But they are so tempting, even if he is an immigrant.'

'Shut up boy! And put that back, will you!' stormed Gauvin.

DI Dalton carefully replaced Kali and raised his hands to remonstrate. 'Please let me put your mind at rest, Sir.'

PS Harris felt his muscles tense as the detective went on.

'I suspect that every artefact here is either smuggled or a forgery, and none of it came from a Mogul palace. Your ancestor wasn't just an adventurer, he was also a crook.'

'Oh shit...' PS Harris groaned audibly as Fitzroy Gauvin went purple with rage at the slander against his illustrious ancestor.

'Oh Daddy!' Connor crowed with sarcastic glee, 'We are free of the curse at last!'

DI Dalton seemed oblivious that the landowner was on the verge of eruption. 'This ceramic of Kali is probably Chinese, made for the European market. Kali is not a vindictive goddess. She was vilified because the Thugs in India worshipped her. Yama would have been a better choice. If you really wanted a potent curse, you didn't need to import one from India. Your ancestors hanged enough herbalists and frail old women as witches to bring down more damnation than any family could cope with.'

'My forebears were God fearing men!"

'Your forebears used the bench to dispose of anyone who challenged their authority, plus a few more who didn't believe in your hellfire and brimstone Church for good measure. They were also slave owners. Google it sometime."

Fitzroy Gauvin looked as though he was about to reach for one of those shotguns PS Harris knew he had licences for.

'Well, thank you for your time, Mr Gauvin,' he declared before his superior could be physically hurled down the mansion's steps, 'we won't take up any more of it.' He placed himself between DI Dalton and the incandescent landowner and shepherded the detective into the hall.

'I'll show them out Daddy.' Connor bounced ahead and led the policemen to the great oak door. 'That was just tremendous, Detective,' he gushed. 'If the old man doesn't have a seizure first he might just get all that junk checked out so at last we can have some real art nouveau or Bauhaus instead. It's so deadly dull having to live amongst all that old pottery and brass.'

'Actually,' interrupted DI Dalton, 'I really wanted to speak to your mother.'

'I think we've outstayed our welcome, Sir,' insisted PS Harris.

'Oh, I'll let her know, Detective. Though there's nothing more she can tell you. I'm pretty sure my brother's meal was spiked at the Curry Palace that evening as well, and Daddy and I don't agree about much.'

'Why so sure?'

'That Bengali waiter has the shiftiest of looks.'

'What motive would he have?'

'Jonah and Daddy have a history of... differences... with the Asian community.'

'Mr Gauvin founded a right-wing party some years ago, Sir,' Harris reminded him.

'Are you two still here!' a voice bellowed from the far end of the hall.

PS Harris fancied he heard cartridges going into a shotgun and shepherded his superior to the car before the air to surface missiles could be launched. Connor stood at the top of the steps waving them off like a string puppet from a children's TV programme.

DI Dalton turned back. 'Bit of a kook, that one.'

PS Harris gripped his arm. 'Let's just keep moving Sir, before Mr Gauvin sends the dogs out.'

'He wouldn't? Would he really?'

The glee in the detective's tone persuaded the sergeant to move even faster, pushing his superior into the passenger seat and slamming the door shut before he could jump back out and enrage the Dobermans as well.

Just as their car reached the end of the drive the sergeant breathed with relief. Then DI Dalton insisted that they stop. Unable to pretend he didn't hear the order, DS Harris reluctantly followed him back through the grounds to the outhouse Connor had initially dashed from.

'This is a very bad idea, Sir! A very bad idea!' hectored PS Harris, all too aware of what a splendid target he would make if those shotguns were loaded.

'It's fine. The dogs are safely inside. You go back and wait in the car.'

PS Harris wanted nothing more than to obey, especially when his superior took a set of lock picks from his jacket and expertly opened the padlock of the outhouse.

'Oh, we are so dead,' murmured Harris.

'It's all right. Won't take a moment.'

With that, DI Dalton pushed the door just wide enough to slip inside. The sergeant could make out that he was examining some chemistry equipment and adding an oily substance to a phial. When finished, the detective poked his head back round the door to ask, 'Did you know that this young man was studying chemistry?'

'Got anything in there for palpitations has he?'

The fuming silence on their return to the station

warned DI Dalton against uttering another word, so he retreated back in his seat to watch the world go by until they arrived.

As soon as he stepped through the door PS Harris could tell by the apprehensive look on PC Wren's face that the furious phone call from Gauvin had preceded them. The chief inspector had demanded to see him immediately.

'I want to apply for armed response duties, Sir,' he declared before he could hear the inevitable reason for him being summoned.

'I thought you hated guns, Harris?'

'I do Sir. I just want to shoot myself.'

There was a brief silence.

'It was that bad, was it?'

'That's not a man! He's a bandicoot!'

'It's all right, Harris. Relax. I just want you to know that you won't be held responsible for anything he does. I can't explain now but, whatever else you do, don't let him out of your sight. You have permission to physically restrain him if necessary.'

'That one would slip out of my grip and disappear through a crack in the floorboards.'

'And Harris ..?' The chief inspector hesitated before asking confidentially, 'Do you think he's gay?'

'Not by the way he's out there flirting with PC Wren. If he is, he's so far back in the closet he should be living in Narnia.'

'Just wondered ...'

Surely nothing could go wrong during their visit to the Curry Palace. Mr Kapoor was a pillar of the community who could read the moods of others as easily as the Puranas. All the same, PS Harris felt tense as he followed DI Dalton through the faux Mogul entrance and past a life-sized image of Shiva.

Although he had not been forewarned of the visit just before lunchtime opening, Mr Kapoor, a friendly man in his mid-40s barely taller than the DI but twice the width, bustled over from the bar at the far end of the restaurant to greet them.

'Sorry to drop in on you unannounced like this, Mr Kapoor,' PS Harris apologised.

'But of course you must if you believe I have poisoned customers, especially ones as illustrious as Mr Gauvin's son.'

'Did you?' demanded DI Dalton. 'The man is a racist, and his eldest son was probably just as bad.'

PS Harris' soul sank, even though the proprietor took the accusation in his stride.

'It is true that Mr Gauvin is a very unpleasant man, but if I had done such a thing it would have been for the benefit of his wife, a wonderful woman with so much to put up with.'

'What about his youngest son?'

'A little strange perhaps, somehow detached from the tribulations of us minor mortals.'

'You mean spaced out on drugs?'

'Not ones I am familiar with, I assure you.'

'DI Knowles ran all the tests and ruled out any contamination in Mr Kapoor's kitchen,' PS Harris reminded the DI. 'If Jonah Gauvin's death was due to a toxin, it could have been administered by anyone.'

Mr Kapoor's face lit up as he realised something. 'Ah, of course! You are DI Dalton!'

'Sorry,' the detective apologised. 'Most people want to hit me before I have chance to introduce myself.'

'I understand that you come from the same town as my wife's mother. You must meet her.'

DI Dalton hesitated as though caught out in some childish prank. 'Of course.'

'A large Indian community lives there and they have this splendid temple,' Mr Kapoor explained to PS Harris.

'Indeed they do,' agreed the DI, 'I have visited it on several occasions.

Then, when PS Harris thought he had been disconcerted enough for one day, DI Dalton started to speak fluent Hindi, much to the delight of Mr Kapoor. He took the detective by the arm for a tour of his restaurant, its sumptuous fittings illuminated in the half light, ready to be turned up as lunch time approached.

When they were out of earshot PS Harris asked the waiter setting tables, 'Know what that's all about, Nabin?'

'I have no idea Mr Harris. I am from Bengal. Though I have a feeling Mr Kapoor's mother-in-law will enter at any second.'

Though she did not speak English, Mrs Prasad was a formidable woman and her talent for managing the restaurant's presentation remarkable. There was never a stain on the starched napkins, wilting flower on the tables or mote of dust on the peacock feathers.

Having completed the tour of his emporium, Mr Kapoor brought his visitor back. And just as the main lights went up Mrs Prasad appeared through the bead curtain that concealed the kitchen door. She immediately studied the restaurant for the slightest imperfection. Nabin flinched at the prospect of her spotting a misplaced fork.

Inspection complete, her gaze fell on the visitors. She knew PS Harris well enough and nodded in acknowledgement.

Then Mrs Prasad saw DI Dalton.

She stood stock still for a moment, unable to look away. Her heavily made up eyes widened then, without explanation, she backed through the curtain and disappeared from sight.

'I know she can be a bit odd at times,' said PS Harris when they had returned to the car, 'but I've no idea what that was all about.'

If he had, it was obvious that DI Dalton wasn't

going to explain.

'Well, where to now, Sir?'

DI Dalton steepled his fingers thoughtfully. 'I think it's about time I paid a visit to a local drug dealer.'

It was inevitable he would get round to asking something like that. 'Cannabis or cocaine?'
'The one least likely to cut our throats.'

'That would be Tim, purveyor of legal highs, under the counter prescription drugs, and brewer of strange substances.'

PS Harris knew it was a mistake to let DI Dalton go into the dilapidated basement by himself, but one glimpse of a policeman's boot through the skylight and the weasel would have fled out of the back door. And Tim was harmless enough, too mellow on his own potions to do much harm. Even his weedy superior could have pushed him over.

The dimly lit steps led down to a rabbit warren of small rooms where odours, fragrant and peculiar, circulated from flasks and trays of drying substances.

Tim, gaunt and woolly-hatted, was so focused on the preparation before him he didn't notice DI Dalton silently enter and look over his shoulder. The visitor at least had the good manners to wait until he had counted the drops from a pipette.

'Interesting smell. Illegal high?'

The pipette almost jumped out of Tim's grasp as

he spun round, wondering how anyone could have entered without activating the alarm's pressure pad under the hall mat.

He quickly recovered. 'Worm potion for the sister's dog. Who the hell are you?'

'Just another copper, but don't worry about it. This is a social call.'

Tim half believed him and didn't feel threatened by this small, stiff man in an immaculate suit and tipped back trilby. In the dim light he could have been taken for one of his more upmarket student customers.

'What can I do for you?'

DI Dalton took out his smartphone and showed it to him. 'He one of yours?'

'Who's asking?'

'Just a friendly pixie who doesn't carry handcuffs.'

'I'll deny it if this is entrapment. But yeah, he cooks up concoctions and experiments with stuff. Studying chemistry he says, though seems to spend too much time away with the fairies to be any good at it.'

'Especially the green ones.'

'Oh Gord. If he's brewing up wormwood and cutting my powders into that muck he's really asking for trouble.'

'You have no idea.' DI Dalton slipped the smartphone back into his pocket. 'Now, I need something for a good night's sleep.'

'See your doctor.'

'I'm not allowed sleeping tablets.'

'What do you think I've got?'

'Something to scare off the night terrors.'

'I've got a few Seroquel. They help customers having bad trips. I can't let you have more than 25 mg. Knowing my luck you might not wake up.'

'Oh, blissful oblivion should be that easy.'
Tim quickly summed up his customer. 'You're only getting two. You'll have to come back if you want any more.'

DI Dalton took a £10 note from his wallet. 'I'll appreciate anything that calms the demon.'

Tim reached for a box and removed a couple of tablets from it. 'And tell PC plod out there that his fat arse should lurk where the big dealers are.'

'He frightens their big, unfriendly dogs.' DI Dalton handed over the money. 'Pleasure doing business with you, Tim.'

'Well let's keep this between us.'

'I won't tell if you don't.'

PS Harris pretended not to notice the small sachet DI Dalton pushed into an inside pocket as he came out and manufactured a conversation to distract himself from what was really going on.

'So Mrs Prasad comes from your neck of the woods then, Sir?'

'Evidently. It's a large town. Somebody has to.'

'PC Wren found this blog mentioning a young copper there. He dashed into a blazing house to save a family. It happened over 20 years ago and she couldn't find a name for him, though I suppose it would be on his death certificate somewhere on our database.'

'They called him Maderu Verma.' There was tedium in the DI's tone, as though the subject had been broached once too often.

'Yeah, the blogger mentioned that.'

'If she must know, his real name was Rupert, or at least that was the one the nurse looking after the newborn gave him - apparently after Rupert Bear. Barnardos added a Smith later.'

'Must've been one hell of a man. Didn't he get a posthumous award?'

The obvious admiration in the sergeant's tone seemed to annoy the DI. 'That would have done him about as much good as a new name.'

PS Harris detected the hardening in his mercurial superior's attitude. 'Poor bugger, I say. Not surprised they treat him like some sort of god.'

'I have a problem with gods.' Then DI Dalton announced without warning, 'I was adopted.'

'That so? How old were you?'

'21.'

PS Harris wanted nothing more than to get home that evening. His daughter's cooking and pint at the local would help distract him from the day's nonsense. So, as per instructions, he ensured that DI Dalton was safely in his hotel room working with his forensic kit before leaving. He had been tempted to lock him in, but even this menace to his peace of mind was entitled to go downstairs for an evening meal.

Braced for the escort duties of following day, PS Harris arrived early at the station. Their usual unmarked car wasn't there, so he assumed somebody else had taken it out.

PC Wren looked up from the front desk. 'Hello Sarge, didn't expect to see you here?'
PS Harris was puzzled. 'What?'
'Just as well you are, though. Mr Kapoor and his mum-in-law say they want to see you urgently. They've been here since six.'

There were two anxious expressions watching from the waiting area so he immediately went over to them.

'What's the problem, Mr Kapoor?'
'I hope this means nothing, but my wife's mother is insistent that there is something you should know.'
'About the Gauvin case?'
'No. About DI Dalton.'

PS Harris' soul had thought it could sink no lower. Nightmare scenarios of what the DI had been up to behind his back flashed through his mind. PC

Wren noticed the change in his expression. She watched from the other side of the glass partition as Mr Kapoor translated what Mrs Prasad had to say.

Harris's expression was so thunderous when he stormed back to the desk she daren't ask what it was.

'Where is he?!' he demanded.

'DI Dalton took the car. I assumed he was going to pick you up.'

'Like hell he was! Did he say where he was going?'

'There was a call from Mrs Gauvin just as Mr Kapoor arrived. She said he wanted to talk to her, so I texted the DI and he came in straight away. Is there anything wrong Sarge?'

'Where that man is concerned, everything is wrong. I need a car.'

'AD55 is waiting outside.' She handed him the keys. 'Shall I tell anyone else?'

'The chief inspector.'

'It's still early.'

'Then wake him up!'

Harris dashed out, followed by Mr Kapoor and Mrs Prasad.

The early morning mist was just lifting when DI Dalton arrived. He left the car at the end of the Gauvin's drive and cut across the grounds to the small pavilion where a frail, yet elegant, woman was waiting for him.

'Are you sure about this?' he asked.

Mrs Gauvin hesitated. 'You should not have come alone. My husband is unbalanced and ceased to know right from wrong years ago.'

'So he hadn't always been delusional?'

'My eldest son was worse. It was probably hereditary.'

'Your youngest son?'

'It's difficult to tell.'

'You do know that he's hooked on wormwood concoctions spiced with other drugs, don't you?'

'That would account for his behaviour.'

'And that he probably poisoned your eldest son's curry with thujone?'

Mrs Gauvin wasn't surprised. 'They did hate each other. I expected Jonah to kill Connor first.' She fastened her jacket and came down from the pavilion to lead DI Dalton across the lawn.

'I'm glad you feel confident enough to do this,' he told her.

'Not many people dare confront my husband in the way you did. But then, that was merely a ploy to reassure me, wasn't it?'

'You'd hardly risk confiding in an investigator who ran away.'

Mrs Gauvin turned to give the detective a reproachful look. 'DI Knowles had no idea of what is really going on, had he?'

'Pity that. He's twice my size and would have dismantled the place, with or without a search warrant. Dinosaurs do have their uses.'

'He wouldn't have found anything, even if he had managed to get past the dogs.'

She pointed to the entrance of an ancient sunken vault overhung by the branches of a Lebanon cedar. A padlock secured its wrought iron gate.

'You will need bolt cutters.'

'A puny mortal like me can barely handle nail clippers.' The detective took out his lock picks.

'Whatever you do, be quick. My husband might not be up yet, but if he does find either of us here he will shoot us.'

DI Dalton easily removed the padlock on the gate, but the heavy metal door beyond it required an authorised fingerprint. Mrs Gauvin watched in bemused surprise as he took a small pad of foam from an inside pocket and pressed it against the security scanner.

He gave a boyish smile. 'Discovered who installed your husband's security. It's baffling why a locksmith would believe it safe to back up his accounts on the Cloud.' With a low whirr the door of the vault yawned opened. 'Now please go to my car and wait there. It's parked at the far end of the drive.'

'I cannot leave you here by yourself. You must call for backup.'

'It's all right. I'm not what you think I am.'

'I think that you are a small, very intelligent man with no sense of danger or bullet-proof vest.'

'Nasty things. They ruin the line of your suit. This won't take a moment.'

Mrs Gauvin peered inside the vault. She had always been aware of what was stored beneath the house, though had never set eyes on it. Now she could see shelves of enough ordnance to supply the small army which the ringleaders of her husband's faction were preparing to mobilise. 'This group are very dangerous men. Jonah was a mere cog fronting the organisation that threatens the security of this country, while my husband dwindled into a witless puppet of the monster he had created.'

'That's why I'm here.'

'Just you? I don't understand?'

'I removed a list of the ringleaders' phone numbers from inside the ceramic of Kali when I examined her. I'm very good at picking pockets as well.'

Mrs Gauvin caught her breath. 'How did you know he kept one there?'

'Fortuitousness. It was also a hunch triggered by a guilty man's body language when I approached her. Even an unbalanced conspirator would know better than to save information like that on an electronic file, and he sincerely believed that this deity would safeguard it. The borderline insane are often persuaded that the world shares their delusions. I don't miss much.' The detective glanced up at the small light flashing above him. 'I did miss that, however.'

'He must know we're here! We have to leave immediately!'

'Just coming.' DI Dalton quickly took several snaps with his smartphone of the vault interior and pulled the door to. It locked with a click and he replaced the padlock on the outer gate. 'You'll have to come with me. It's obvious you aren't safe.'

Mrs Gauvin was following him to the car when a penetrating voice cut through the early morning air. 'Mummy! Mummy! What are you doing out here? Daddy wants to know where you are!'

'Please be quiet Connor!'

But the young man was still addled by the experimental toxins of the previous night and didn't register the urgency in her tone.

Then there was the desperate voice of Cameron, the butler, remonstrating with Fitzroy Gauvin as he stormed from the house.

Connor was confused. 'Oh look, here comes Daddy now. Why's he carrying that shotgun?'

It was too late to run. Gauvin had his wife and the detective in range and could have easily gunned down both of them.

DI Dalton placed himself in front of Mrs Gauvin and Connor became hysterical as the seriousness of the situation overwhelmed the effects of the drugs.

'I think Daddy's very angry, Mummy! What have you been doing? You aren't really going to shoot Mummy, are you Daddy?'

'I should have known no copper could be as stupid as you?' bellowed Gauvin. 'Who sent you? Special Branch? Fat lot of good that will do when we've taken out the major institutions! Then the country will dance to our tune! Too many people are on our side for you to do anything about it now!'

'We know the ringleaders, Mr Gauvin. Shooting me or your wife will not alter that.'

'Please Sir!' Cameron called from a safe distance. 'Please think about what you are doing!' When it was obvious that wasn't going to happen, he took a mobile from his pocket and dialled. 'Try not to move, Mrs Gauvin! I'm calling for help!'

Fitzroy Gauvin's tumultuous thoughts made him deaf to the entreaties of his butler, screeching of his son, and slam of a car door a short distance away. He was only aware of the insolent non-entity who had sent his aspirations of so many years plummeting into the abyss of lost causes.

DI Dalton could see the man's world crashing about him. Then, before commonsense was able to stop him, that demon in his soul taunted, 'Forget Kali! This small god has got your numbers! All of them!'

There was a report from the shotgun.

Its cartridge struck DI Dalton with a sickeningly

hollow thud and lifted the small man like a paper bag snatched up by a gust of wind.

As Gauvin discharged the second barrel a large figure came between them and took the full force of the blast.

The wind knocked out of him, PS Harris looked down at the shredded surface of his protective vest and then at the pistol Gauvin pulled from his belt as he dropped the shotgun.

Connor was sure the policeman turned green with rage, and not into the absinthe fairy he was so familiar with. With a bellow of fury that reverberated about the grounds, this incredible hulk launched himself at Gauvin, landing a huge fist on his jaw, breaking it, and then snatched up the shotgun to smash its butt into the side of his head.

Seeing his father laying motionless, Connor shrieked in terror and ran off.

'Officer down! Officer down! Shots fired! Need medics and backup!' Harris shouted into his radio.

Help instantly appeared in the form of Mr Kapoor and Mrs Prasad who had driven across the lawn and pulled up by the police car.

'We need something to staunch the blood!' Mrs Gauvin called. 'He's bleeding terribly!'

'There are some clean napkins in the boot,' Mr Kapoor remembered, but Mrs Prasad had already opened it and snatched a handful.

Mrs Gauvin tried to loosen DI Dalton's tie. He

seized her hand and refused to release her. But Cameron was immediately there. He expertly slipped the jacket from the detective's shoulders and unbuttoned the blood drenched shirt to expose the wound. This also revealed something else Mrs Gauvin and the butler had not been prepared for. She gave a small cry of horror and recoiled, while he allowed PS Harris to take his place.

Mrs Prasad quickly handed him the napkins and then tried to calm Mrs Gauvin.

What they were looking at came as no surprise to her.

DI Dalton managed to focus on the man who had tried to save his life. 'You're mad at me, aren't you?'

'Of course I am, you daft little sod!' The DI started to lose consciousness so PS Harris shouted. 'Oh no you don't! You stay with us!'

Cameron brought some blankets and they attempted to keep the detective conscious until the ambulance arrived, which was rapidly followed by armed response, local police and senior officers.

The paramedic took one look at DI Dalton's wound.

She called to her ambulance care assistant, 'He's losing blood and going into shock!'

The two women frantically tried to stabilise the patient.

Eventually the paramedic stopped and shook her head.

'I'm sorry. He's gone.' She turned to the large police officer clutching the detective's hand and still talking to him. 'What was his name?'

PS Harris didn't respond, so Mr Kapoor stepped forward.

He respectfully brought his hands together and inclined his head. 'His name, madam, was Maderu Verma.'

Print Out Your Pet

'Hey Terry, come and see this.'

Terry left the file he was working on and went over to view the monitor Tyrone was gazing at.

'Good God! What the hell is that!'

'Must be a rubber toy of some sort. Think I should print it out?'

'Well the bloke paid for it online - don't see how you can't. Apart from that, we've already done that one of the bloke mooning at the scanner, so we can hardly turn this one down. How large does he want it?'

'Life-size.'

'You've got to be joking...' Terry wandered back to his workstation and Tyrone sent the file to the 3-D printer.

This one must have come into the supermarket early while they were busy stocking the shelves, otherwise somebody would have noticed. The creature looked too real to be a toy, and it was unlikely any manufacturer would have produced something that scared the wits out of infants. It was anyone's guess what it was meant to be.

Every now and then Terry stopped adding colour to the customers he was working on in Sense to watch in disbelief as the gruesome, corgi-sized shapie was replicated, layer by layer, pixel by scary pixel. It had fangs, short bat-like wings, a crest of spines, and four dumpy legs supporting it like a wonky coffee table.

No, that certainly wasn't a toy.

Tracey wondered why all the other checkouts still had their queues while customers were suddenly avoiding hers. Perhaps the hair lacquer she had overdone that morning was driving away asthma sufferers. Then she became aware of a tall man in an ankle length cloak looking down at her. She could have sworn that only seconds ago he had been several aisles away.

He held out the receipt for a 3-D shapie.

This customer was creepy and she wanted to tell him that he was at the wrong till but, "**Go to any checkout**" in bold letters was on the bottom of the receipt.

Tracey tapped in the order number and hit *collect*.

It seemed to take forever for the item to arrive. When it eventually did, the shapie was in a large, sealed cardboard box.

Marion placed it on the track, casting the sinister man an apprehensive glance before examining the receipt as though it was impregnated with a fatal toxin.

This was going to be one of those strange mornings, Tracey decided. They happened every now and then regardless of what precautions you took. Smiling sweetly did not always deter awkward customers, though this one was politeness personified. He even dipped a courteous bow as he accepted his shapie. Most of them came in cellophane so the customer could see the result. They could be grateful, pleasantly surprised, or downright offended that any machine possessed the temerity to destroy the image they had of themselves.

As this customer pulled the tape from his box with immaculately manicured, long nails Tracey was aware of something snuffling and grunting under the hem of his cloak. With the checkout track separating them, it was impossible to see what it was.

Just wishing the man would go, she watched him take out the scale model of a hideous creature in black, red and silver.

Tracey may have worked in a supermarket, but knew enough history to realise that centuries ago people really did believe in the Devil and his familiars. Perhaps the man had brought in some ancient heirloom to replicate for insurance purposes.

The customer gave another polite bow, placed the model back in its box and swept towards the supermarket entrance with it tucked under his arm.

Only then did Tracey see why people were backing away to let him pass.

On a silver lead, waddling happily by his side, was the creature he had brought in to replicate. Pets were not allowed on the premises, but neither of the store's security men had offered to point this out to him.

The sinister man's companion was squat, mumbling away to itself through fearsome looking fangs, and flapping its short stubby wings as though in frustration at knowing that they would never manage to lift it from the ground.

Modesty Wear

Bella had always been easily embarrassed and since childhood avoided the critical glances of other people.

There was no reason for her to do this; she was an extraordinarily attractive 21-year-old and, the more beautiful she became, the more she felt the need to conceal the fact. Unfortunately Bella had no religious commitment to hide her modesty behind. All the veils, hijabs, shifts and ankle length habits were the preserve of nuns, Islam and the Amish.

To make matters worse, she now yearned to go swimming.

On the beach floaty sarongs and tissue thin garments were removed to reveal skimpy bikinis verging on the illegal, even if the wearers were 16 stone and in their fifties. They should have provided enough distraction for Bella to slip into the water unnoticed - or would have done if she had not been over six foot tall. Even in a one-piece swimsuit she would have been far too self conscious, yet wearing modesty swimwear would have probably attracted even more attention. Surely there was some costume she could feel comfortable in without looking like a Victorian matron descending the steps of a bathing machine on Brighton beach.

Bella went online yet again and searched for swimwear that looked attractive, wasn't only available in the US, and came in her inconvenient size. There was nothing. Stunningly attractive, six-foot two tall young women apparently only existed in films or fashion magazines. As much as Bella aspired to be a model, the thought of quick changes in communal dressing rooms filled her with dread. It was something she might have overcome in the right environment, but that profession was already filled with underweight teenagers almost as tall as she was.

Bella continued to secretly search online for modesty fashions when no one else in the insurance broker's office was watching when, one day, up popped something quite unexpected. It was an ornate, gold edged invitation to view a parade of designs which celebrated the female human form by enveloping it in sumptuous fabrics. Linked to it were one or two pictures that triggered her interest. This designer understood Bella's dilemma perfectly in creating costumes for all occasions - including the swimming pool.

Convinced that it was all quite genuine, she hit PayPal to purchase the invitation and was sent a PDF to print out and present at the entrance.

It was a beautiful day to stroll across the immaculately manicured lawn of the Georgian mansion where the longest catwalk Bella had ever seen had been installed. There was seating along its full length yet, despite the admittance fee being in aid of the local church restoration fund, the audience was small. The reason why was explained in the brochure handed to Bella.

Apparently Malcolm Marconitti had an eccentric reputation that deterred high street clothes shops and other fashion outlets from stocking his creations and persuaded the buyers for major supermarkets to block his emails. Even critics and the local press failed to turn up. This was not something the clothes designer needed to worry about. He owned the Georgian mansion and funds to indulge his creative muse. Though it apparently hadn't occurred to him to spend some of that fortune raising the profile of the Marconitti website. Even Bella couldn't believe that he intended to send models wearing this extraordinary, and downright impossible, collection shown in the brochure down that long catwalk covered in fuchsia coloured felt so she sat tight in anticipation. This was more exhilarating than searching for modesty swimwear on the Internet.

Malcolm Marconitti, individualist and creator of the outrageous, strutted out like an effete ostrich to briefly explain his vision of what the world should be wearing. Over his carmine hair was a headdress sprouting ostrich feathers and trimmed with sequinned ribbons fluttering like pennants in the breeze. In a welter of adjectives and adverbs with very few nouns, hands in non-stop semaphore, he explained the inspiration for his creations. Surprisingly, mind-bending drugs were not involved; the eccentric gene ran in the family.

Presentation over, he stepped aside to allow his statuesque models onto the catwalk.

The parade began modestly with those neat, colourful swimsuits similar to the ones Bella had been attracted to on the US websites. She hoped they weren't prohibitively expensive because, given the height of the models, they must have come in her size. They were followed by full-length gowns for the beach which floated like huge butterflies trying to get airborne.

On the other side of the fluttering silk, Bella noticed an older woman glancing in her direction. Her lantern-jawed features and magnetic expression suggested that she wielded authority in Malcolm Marconitti's entourage and may have been scrutinising the sparse audience for potential customers.

Bella forgot about her as soon as outfits, which would have filled the court of Madame Pompadour with apprehension, issued from the marquee, their hummingbird headdresses fluttering as though in triumph at achieving flight. Layered crinoline skirts swirled, dervish like, about the models and tasselled sleeves described satin circles with every movement.

Surely nothing could follow that. Then out came a line of pagoda like creations. Shoulder pads swept up like ornamental ridges were topped by dragons breathing flame. Despite the fire risk, a small devil inside Bella wished that she could wear something like it - however embarrassing, even though there would never be a suitable occasion, apart from Mardi Gras or the circus. She was so overwhelmed by Malcolm Marconitti's extraordinary vision that all thoughts of modesty swimwear evaporated. Bella should have winced when the impractical and outrageous gave way to the downright implausible and dangerous. Instead she was desperate to see more.

The next models did not stride along the catwalk; they floated above it like gossamer kites embellished with sequins. Bella could hardly believe her eyes. Surely Health and Safety - or even Air-sea Rescue - would dash in and put an end to the extravaganza at any moment. But who cared as the fearless models manoeuvred their fantastic costumes several feet above the ground using fans as ailerons.

Bella wanted to be up there with them. Forget swimming: flying through the air like a huge, glittering kite had not been on her list of things to do before reaching 30 - now it was at the top. Despite her innate modesty, Bella knew that she was just as tall and good looking as Malcolm Marconitti's models.

When it seemed as if things could not get any more thrilling there was a commotion from the far end of the catwalk. And it was not Health and Safety or Air-sea Rescue. A delegation of severely dressed men and women was descending on the fashion parade like acolytes of some vengeful deity. If Malcolm Marconitti was gloriously eccentric, these representatives from Hades were conformity at its most narrow-minded. Nothing like this could have happened at any other fashion parade, however provoking the costumes. Had this designer managed, by sheer force of imagination, to arouse the ire of agents dedicated to the suppression of visionaries? Was this a regular occurrence? And, if so, why had such peculiar goings-on not appeared on the Internet?

One of the sinister battalion snatched the frame containing the floatation cells of a hovering model and tried to pull her from the sky. This upset her buoyancy and she ascended higher, taking the assailant with her. They were soon out of reach, sailing towards the neighbouring village as she beflaboured the man with her steel ribbed fan.

Malcolm Marconitti, his entourage, and the straight-laced delegation dashed out of the grounds and down the lane after the model and her assailant.

The pair came to rest on the roof of the parish church.

Their pursuers arrived in time to see a furious vicar and congregation spill out from the middle of a baptism to join the extraordinary melee.

Amazingly no one had been hurt.

Despite herself, Bella doubled up with laughter. Who were all these ridiculous people? Was she dreaming?

She felt a discreet hand on her arm.

The lantern-jawed woman she had seen earlier was holding a finger to her lips.

Bella choked back her laughter. 'What is going on?'

'Our visitors are Mr Marconitti's relatives, who believe they have a claim to his estate on the grounds of his insanity, and their legal representatives. Descending on his fashion parades without warning to provoke such situations is one of the ways they hope to persuade a court that he is certifiable.'

'But his clothes are glorious,' protested Bella. 'How could anybody believe they were designed by a madman?'

'It would not be the first time that imagination has been declared a sign of insanity. We would like to laugh as well, but the loss if his remarkable creations due to the bigotry of an avaricious family would not be so amusing.'

Bella was indignant. 'You should start an online campaign to promote his work. The world would soon decide who was right.'

The woman shook her head. 'Mr Marconitti has always resisted publicity.'

They watched as the vicar, obviously familiar with his neighbour's eccentricities, turned his attention to the delegation that had disrupted the fashion parade. With one of their number stranded on the roof and still being belaboured by the model, and an extended family trying to calm a screeching baby, he made it known in no uncertain terms that greed was a venal sin and would be repaid in Hell. Mr Malcolm Marconitti was a good and generous man, and deserved more respect for the worthy causes he donated money to.

While the argument between Church and lawyers droned on, Bella turned to the lantern-jawed woman and asked, 'You don't need another model do you? Women my height attract too much attention to have fun, and working in an insurance office can be soul destroying. Life would be far more interesting if I could fly in one of those wonderful outfits.'

'And this hasn't put you off?'

'On the contrary, it has opened up vistas I would never have dreamt of.'

'I shall recommend you to Mr Marconitti. Just be sure to draw up your own insurance policy before you join us.'

The Cult of the Cosmic Egg

'Of course, they're all using it as an excuse to have a quiet drink together. And if they aren't, they're all quite batty. "Cult of the Cosmic Egg" indeed! At least you've got to give them full marks for originality. My mum is just glad that granddad has found something to keep him occupied, even if it is an excuse to roll home inebriated at 11 o'clock. Pity I haven't got any pictures to post. I'd love to see this wonderful Cosmic Egg. Perhaps Trini will do a painting of it next time the nursery gets out the paints.'

Joanne closed her Facebook page. It was time to go and meet her boyfriend in the local Pizza Hut.

Her granddad and his mates were in a more private venue, the room above the saloon bar of the Happy Hen. The pub used to be called The Royal, but the new landlord was a republican and kept chickens: one of the rare occasions when it wasn't possible to blame a major brewery for allocating it one of those silly names they were so enamoured of at one time. This was a free house and Ron brewed his own ale, much appreciated by the locals even if he was anti-royalist.

The members of the Cult of the Cosmic Egg were so far; Herbert, a banker on the cusp of retirement;

Julian, a chemistry teacher who should have known better than to declare a belief in such things; Algernon, the rotund baker forever coming up with more options for greasy, sweet pastries; John, who could never get a word in edgeways because of his stammer and unable to walk without crutches; and Jerry, Joanne's grandfather.

Their meetings started out with a discussion about the plausibility of the Cosmic Egg to impress the staff and customers downstairs who could hear most of what was going on through the low ceiling. Not that any of them were fooled for one moment. The meetings soon dwindled into exchanges of dirty jokes and arguments about more earthly matters like politics, allotment management and the colour of the barmaid's underwear. While they put the world to rights, Ron kept them well supplied with the house brew. When the tenuous link with weighty matters had dissolved in the alcoholic haze they eventually wended their ways home under the impression they had spent a productive evening, even if none of them could remember all of it.

One evening, the Cult of the Cosmic Egg had hardly touched their first jar when there was a rap at the door. It was too soon for their second ale so Julian, half expecting that a student had tracked him down, jumped up to open it, well armed with an excuse about exploring cosmic chemistry. Far from it being a pupil wanting to know why this respected teacher had aligned himself to such a ludicrous premise as the Universe hatching cosmic anomalies, it was a total stranger wearing a long orange robe and carrying a staff. He had coal black eyes which glinted sinisterly in the light of the faux Tiffany wall lights. Despite his usual loquacity, Julian was lost for words.

'Can I help you, mate?' Jerry called from his chairman's seat at the head of the table.

Two deathly white hands appeared from the cuffs of the stranger's robe. He raised them, palms up as though able to catch the question. 'I understand from the proprietor that you are the Cult of the Cosmic Egg?'

Julian remained speechless. Nobody had ever been taken in by the topers' pretence to have a few ales in private, let alone believe that there was such a thing as the Cosmic Egg.

'That's right,' Herbert replied authoritatively, totally unabashed by its absurdity.

'How did you find out?' Julian at last asked, trying not to sound too surprised.

'There were some interesting entries on Facebook.'

Jerry groaned. 'I'll throttle that little madam,' he muttered under his breath.

'Don't you mind us, mate,' the jolly Algernon called out. 'You come in and join us if you like.'

As nobody else objected, Julian stood aside to let

the stranger enter. 'Pull up a chair.'

Then something occurred to Algernon. 'I bet you're a teetotaller, aren't you?'

The stranger nodded.

'W... w... w... well I hope you won't m... m... mind us drinking?' said John. 'It cures m... m... my stammer.'

'Of course not. I would never dream of expecting others to share my self-disciplines.' The stranger sat in the chair Julian indicated, facing the head of the table.

None of them had encountered a committed believer in anything much before - at least not one that was genuine, and there was something so intriguing about the stranger they had to take him seriously. Julian assumed, by the orange robe, that he was a Buddhist, which in his eyes was more worthwhile than many other beliefs. The others knew little about what that entailed, so weren't going to embarrass the man by enquiring.

But Herbert asked the visitor, as though he was applying for a bank loan, who he was and to explain why he found their little club so interesting.

The stranger's name was Ranulph. Meditation had opened up the capacity for him to appreciate all other beliefs, however unlikely. The Cult of the Cosmic Egg particularly intrigued him for some reason he declined to explain because he doubted that its members believed it.

The apprehensive silence they maintained on the subject confirmed his suspicion. So Ranulph invited the drinking companions to look a little deeper than the bottom of their ale glasses and explore the wonder of the Cosmos through meditation.

Julian was all too willing, if only to satisfy his scientific curiosity, though the others had reservations about meddling with the mellow state of mind they really aspired to.

After the number of businesses Herbert had condemned to liquidation by refusing them loans he was reluctant to delve into his subconscious that deeply - there slept Marley's ghost! Algernon just couldn't see the point. He was happy enough in his calorific world and fully expected to find out what it was all about eventually anyway when the inevitable heart attack sent him to the great bakery in the sky. John would have liked to try it, but it would have been impossible for him to sit cross-legged, and the Happy Hen's house brew cured his stammer.

Jerry - well Jerry - it only took him a couple of seconds to mull anything over before jumping in with both feet. 'Can we have a few more jars before we do this?'

'Meditation works best when the mind is clear, but I appreciate someone attempting this for the first time might need a little "lubrication" to help them relax,' Ranulph conceded.

'And this really isn't the place. With all that din

going on downstairs it would be difficult to focus,' said Julian. 'Perhaps we should go to the garden by the canal. It's very quiet at this time of evening and there's enough lighting to prevent anyone from falling in.'

Herbert and Algernon made it clear that they were only prepared to be interested onlookers, and reluctantly agreed to join the others.

So they had two more ales and, slightly inebriated, the Cult of the Cosmic Egg wended its way down the stairs and out through the back door of the Happy Hen.

As they reached the wild flowers planted by a local school on the bank of the canal, John found his enthusiasm increasing and he settled down on a child-sized bench. The others sat on the grass around him and endeavoured not to look too ridiculous, adamantly refusing to adopt the lotus position and look mystical.

Ranulph sat facing them, elegantly positioning himself like a guru. He explained how they should close their eyes and push away all the intrusive thoughts that clogged up the mind and made existence so complicated.

Ranulph's quiet commitment impressed Algernon and Herbert enough for them to condescendingly try it. Their meditation lasted for a few brief moments before thoughts came back to continue transforming their grey matter to blancmange, helped by the ale and fact it was fast approaching their bedtimes. Algernon toppled over backwards and fell fast asleep, closely followed by Herbert. Unable to ignore the bank manager's undignified snoring, John also felt himself dosing and, with a stammered apology, fell sideways onto the bench and into the arms of Morpheus.

That left just Julian and Jerry facing Ranulph. The mystic did not seem disconcerted that his erstwhile pupils had fallen so quickly at the first hurdle. He raised his hands to the overcast sky murmuring some inaudible incantation.

A ghostly circle began to form on the bank of the canal just below them. It resembled the shape of an egg, growing larger and larger until it opened a glowing tunnel into light filled infinity.

Jerry and Julian knew that they had to be dreaming and it was time to wake up, but the drinking partners were mesmerised as they gazed down the throat of this otherworldly dimension.

'I really think this ought to stop now,' Julian tried to say, but the words would not come.

Ranulph continued his incantation until the egg-shaped portal was large enough for a man to step through.

Then the mystic rose, his orange robe floating about him in the cosmic light like an unfurling lotus. 'This is the gateway to all things. Creation was born through these doorways from other universes. We all come from the atoms shared between dimensions.'

At last Julian managed to speak and sound reasonably sensible. 'You're really talking about quantum mechanics, aren't you?'

'This is your perception. There are many layers to reality. The human mind can only comprehend one.' Ranulph beckoned Julian and Jerry to follow him into the anomaly.

Julian wasn't that drunk and firmly refused.

But Jerry was game for anything. That had always been his problem. It was a wonder he had survived into his seventies.

He got up and followed Ranulph into infinity.

When Julian woke he only had a vague recollection of the egg-shaped portal. Neither he, John, Algernon, nor Herbert were willing to admit that they had woken in the early hours by the canal, soaked to the skin by overnight rain, and mentioned what had happened to no one.

Joanne and her mother soon realised that Jerry was not coming home and started to make enquiries. The other members of the Cult of the Cosmic Egg believed that their shared experience had been a hallucination and still refused to admit it could have been anything else, though it would have made some sort of horrible sense. They could only conjecture that Ranulph had spiked their ale and persuaded Jerry to walk into the canal in the belief he was entering another plane of existence. Of course, Julian did not suggest to his daughter and granddaughter that he had drowned, though mentioned to the police that they had often strolled along the canal after a few drinks and he might have been swept over the weir into the next county.

None of them expected to see Ranulph again, especially as they were on the verge of convincing themselves that he had been a figment of their imaginations.

But one lunchtime Justin and Herbert walked into the saloon bar of the Happy Hen for a quick bite to eat - and there he was - serving ale!

But was it Ranulph? Ron introduced him as his new partner in the brewing business. The man they had encountered was teetotal and had irises as black as coal. This Ranulph's eyes were pale grey. He wore a tartan shirt and jeans, not orange robe, and there was no staff in sight, apart from the one Ron kept behind the counter to deal with troublemakers. And, to confound the possibility that this was the culprit who had led Jerry into oblivion, he had a wide, friendly smile which convinced them he was totally oblivious to the doppelgänger who had briefly appeared to show them how to meditate. The nearest this companionable Ranulph would ever get to contemplation was being mesmerised by the foam fermenting on the house brew.

Weeks went by and Joanne began to accept that

she may never see her grandfather again. He had always been a free spirit and often disappeared without warning, but now he was too old to endure the rigours of an outdoor life for any length of time.

The Cult of the Cosmic Egg carried on meeting, and drinking, though would only open the door to Ron. One glance at Ranulph after a few jars might well have sent their inebriated brains spinning away on another trip to Wonderland.

Then one evening there was a rap at the old panelled door. It wasn't the knock Ron used, so they ignored it. It also sounded as though it had been made with the head of a staff.

Then there was a voice they instantly recognised.

Julian leapt up to let Jerry in.

But it was not the Jerry they knew.

His ageing eyes were now coal black, and he wore a long orange robe.

'Of course we're glad to see him back. I don't know what bender he's been on all this time, but he's turned quite peculiar. He swears that this Cult of the Cosmic Egg, which they used as an excuse to drink together, is the real thing. Creation somehow tunnelled from another universe and made the Big Bang, and us, or whatever. It's all above my head. Can't think how he worked it all out. He seems pretty convinced, so we humour him. It's as much as mum can do to stop him taking his staff and orange robe to spread the word to the other pubs in the neighbourhood. And I'm not so sure he still won't take off one night without warning. So, if you do meet my granddad and he starts spouting about the Cosmic Egg, whatever you do - don't let him show you how to meditate!'

Bodkin's Bazaar

Tuppence, real name Alice Ann, had never been interested in world changing events. Wars were boring, ecologists nagged, and climatologists only promised more rain. She much preferred to sit in front of her laptop playing online games or shopping while tucking away ready-made meals loaded with calories. In her favourite fashion outlets customers could wander along virtual aisles stocked with trinkets and tasteless T-shirts. As Tuppence's waistline continued to expand, it was inevitable that the selfie posted on Facebook would attract vindictive messages. Going on a diet was out of the question, and it was a lot easier to close her Facebook account. The young woman's self image was formed by the delusion she would be able to wear all those glamorous gowns and skimpy dresses parading on her monitor.

 One evening, after an exhausting day at the checkout of the supermarket, Tuppence microwaved a new fat laden delicacy that it was promoting and sat down to surf. She had already seen most of the designer clothes, gaudy dress jewellery and outrageous shoes, so typed in "glitter garters bangles" just to see what would come up.

 And something did – "Bodkin's Bazaar".

 The page looked so enticing, with a portal framed by leafy tendrils and overlooked by the slightly sinister face of the Green Man. Hitting "enter" opened the gates of this fantastic market, half antique fair, and half fairyland. The extravagant stalls were laden with lace as fine as cobwebs, bangles and butterfly kites. Glittering kaleidoscopic windmills were being turned by the fluttering wings of fairy attendants offering multicoloured ice cream and marzipan sweets from huge rose petals. Bodkin's Bazaar was a feast for the senses and temptation for the virtual purse.

Tuppence was breathless with excitement. She downloaded the 3-D app the website offered and put on her goggles.

Now firefly lanterns lit the way, illuminating displays of elfin jewellery, gossamer scarves, and bracelets of entwined silver and gold. There was a roundabout with griffins, turtles and unicorns dipping and dancing with no visible signs of support. Tuppence would have been tempted to ride one if there had been something holding them up, but wouldn't have risked it, even in this virtual world. Instead she accepted an ice cream from one of the fairy's petals. She wondered what she would encounter in the fortune teller's tent glowing with astrological symbols. The Bodkin's Bazaar programme no doubt had millions of pre-written predictions for virtual visitors. So she went in.

A willowy man wearing a green robe and a pink turban like a huge bud about to bloom greeted her.

Tuppence started to feel disorientated as she sat before his crystal ball. This dimension was changing and no longer seemed so secure. Tempted to pull off the goggles, the eldritch allure of Bodkin's Bazaar held her fast.

'How does anyone pay for all this?' she wondered out loud, not expecting any reply from the CGI manikin. 'There's no checkout.'

The young man spread his hands. 'All we require is your indulgence.'

Oh no! This should not be happening! Interaction on this level was only possible if someone else shared the programme.

Tuppence panicked and attempted to wrench off the 3D goggles.

They would not budge.

'There is no need to be alarmed. Our software is like no other. Just ask me a question. I will answer it.'

There was only one question. 'What is this place? I thought Bodkin's Bazaar was a market?'

'Goodness no. We have no interest in mortal money.'

'So you don't want anything for telling my fortune?'

'Of course not, I will do that with pleasure. Though yours is too significant for a mere crystal ball. Come with me and view what the future has in store for you.' The young man rose like an unbending sapling and beckoned Tuppence to follow him.

Every fibre of her commonsense vibrating against it, she went out into the fortune teller's magical realm, through the avenues of trinkets tinkling in a rising breeze. The allure of Bodkin's Bazaar now felt sinister and far too exotic, even for an Eastern souk. Tuppence became intoxicated by the perfume of strange spices and too soporific to wonder how anyone could have dreamt of such an extraordinary place. It was another dimension.

A chill of fear made her shudder. 'Where are we?'

'Deep in the wood that will never be.'

'It's like fairyland.'

'This is the magical realm being swallowed by a thoughtless, avaricious species.'

Tuppence realised that the fortune teller was as much sprite as all the other fairies and elves that were peering from the branches and bracken.

They reached a beautiful tree at the centre of Bodkin's Bazaar, pennants of silk fluttering from its branches and crystal wind chimes spinning amongst its leaves. Huge cushions were placed against the roots of the giant oak. Her guide invited her to sit down, and took his place opposite her.

'Now just close your eyes and focus on all those things you hold most dear.'

The dearest things to Tuppence were, in descending order; food, shopping online, her pet Pomeranian and second hand mini. Family and the occasional boyfriend were also there, but quite low down on the list. Although she lived in the same house, parents and siblings had drifted apart like croutons bobbing on the soup of indifference, only to sink before they could be appreciated.

Unable to stop the wonderful pastries, hamburgers and curries swamping her hungry thoughts, she dozed off.

Tuppence expected to wake up in her armchair, laptop on the coffee table and goggles still over her eyes.

But she woke in Bodkin Bazaar's enchanted wood. The cushions and fortune teller had gone and she was sprawled against the roots of that great tree. The oak was now quite dead, its once glorious crown of leaves shrivelled and a heavily polluted, leaden sky louring down at her through its skeletal branches.

Tuppence pushed herself up. The ground felt oily and air was stifling. The woodland that had surrounded Bodkin's Bazaar was now filled with rotting tree stumps.

Overwhelmed by nausea, she once again tried to wrench off the goggles responsible for allowing her into this nightmarish landscape.

They were no longer there.

Close to tears, Tuppence scrambled through the dead undergrowth slippery with toxic substances and up to the brow of a hill where she looked out over an ugly, blighted landscape. Roads that had once crisscrossed the view were now undermined by repeated inundations, and the woods and fields ravaged by catastrophic storms.

There was no birdsong, no cows and sheep grazing on the grey land or sunlight warming the bleak vista. The sun had long since set on this miserable environment, its rays blocked out by the blanket of pollution.

Then there was that blood chilling sound, like the creaking of the branches in the ancient, dead oak tree. In it was a traumatised voice, laughing - or perhaps crying.

'Who are you?' Tuppence sobbed.

The sound grew into the fury of rushing wind from which words gushed. 'We are the victims of your greed and thoughtlessness! We will recover and grow again, but you will be gone forever.'

Tuppence didn't recognise herself in its accusation. She reckoned herself to be a generous soul, never stinting when it came to fundraising, willing to feed anyone's pets while they were away, or even lend a needy friend her eyeliner. How could she be thought of as so greedy and thoughtless?

'I don't understand?' she wailed.

'Don't you drive a car, eat the flesh of animals, squander water and energy, and use the land as though it was a cesspit?'

Tuppence had to admit to the first three, but the cesspit was going too far. She may have dropped the odd piece of litter - by accident of course - but certainly never defecated in public places.

'But everyone drives and eats hamburgers,' she protested. 'Why do I have to be singled out?'

But the voice trailed off with incoherent words, fading back into the creaking branches of the dead tree.

Tuppence's knees buckled as she felt herself falling.

Suddenly she was awake, sprawled on the floor of her bedroom.

Shaking, trying to not cry out for fear of attracting the attention of others in the house, she climbed back into her armchair.

Then she saw the laptop screen.

It had been infected by a virus.

Gazing out at her was a mask like face. But this was not the V for Vendetta disguise. He had leaves for hair and beard, and vines growing from his grinning mouth.

The Green Man was laughing with a deep, vengeful tone full of loathing for humanity.

Live Your Dream

Barry had one moment of glory in his long acting career. It was so long ago few were alive to remember it. Even he was beginning to find that moment of fame on the big screen merging with daydreams and half recalled snapshots of lost glory.

Was it really so long ago? He had been famous for a few precious weeks, only to wind up in a dingy basement flat, riddled with arthritis and type 2 diabetes, forgotten and unemployable. Barry's last role had been in an advert for margarine in which he provided the voice of a cranky cow who resented the oily product. Even if the looks had long disappeared, the voice was still there. During these twilight years his virtually estranged agent would phone on the odd occasion to offer a crumb of comfort in some tiny voice over role for a CGI movie or as the narrator for an inane documentary to be aired on an obscure cable channel.

The more time went by, the more Barry lamented that he had once been on the verge of Hollywood stardom. For one glorious month he had believed his destiny to be with all those other heavenly bodies posing for the cameras and being pursued by the paparazzi of the day. Of course, back then, the film companies kept the private lives of their stars strictly controlled then, but that would have been a small price to pay for immortality. Now, not only was he totally forgotten, he was alone after his long-term partner had succumbed to the ravages of AIDS. Having nursed Jason for so many years, Barry was well aware of how brutal life could be. All the more reason to once again crave communion with that fantasy celluloid world, which had slipped so unfairly from his grasp.

There had been no scandal, no disagreement over the contract with the major studio; just one comment from its mogul that he was "too English". 20th Century Fox had George Saunders, and there was no way Barry could compete with that. So instead they signed up a totally unknown bit part player with the charisma of a rattlesnake and habits of tomcat.

By the time the studio realised their mistake, Barry was well down the slide to obscurity, even depending on income from appearances as a drag queen. Then followed pantomimes and washing up at an upmarket hotel. Only Jason had made it all bearable. Now the bit part player who had snatched stardom from him, the suave George Saunders, and Jason were all dead. Barry had been offered a place in a home for retired performers, but graciously declined, fearful that he would encounter greater names than him who had also fallen on hard times. What could he hope to say to them given their once elevated status? Fortunately he was still mobile and could remember his pin number, if not much else, though the expense of keeping a car and seeing oncoming traffic had become too much so he gave up his driving licence after Jason died. And Barry had his laptop to search for the stars and films of yesteryear.

One evening he sat sipping his gin and tonic, Googling the biographies and film credits of other long forgotten actors in IBMb, when, changing links, an advert popped up from nowhere as though it had detected the yearning in his world-weary soul. Barry may not have been techno-savvy, but the services it offered seemed quite plausible as well as tempting. For a modest fee "Live Your Dream" would, using their newly developed technology, put the customer centre stage of any film, old or new, they chose. With the aid of a harmless opiate, electrodes stimulating selected areas of the brain and images flashed onto the retina, the subject would be able to live with the stars for one glorious hour.

Humphrey Bogart was at the top of Barry's list. He had always been a fan. The man may not have been an astounding actor or handsome, and had troublesome teeth, but his screen presence was unmatched. So what if it did involve cortical stimulation and having images beamed onto the retinas? Given Barry's encroaching forgetfulness and age, there was little that could be done to his brain to make it any less efficient. It might even do it a power of good.

So the veteran actor pulled out his credit card and tapped in its number; £60 for one hour of bliss. Not a bad price to relieve the unremitting dullness of his life.

He printed out his receipt and went to bed reasonably content.

"Live Your Dream" was located in an old disused studio which at one time had half a dozen busy sound stages. It had been easy to reach by train and Barry vaguely remembered performing a small role on at least one of them.

Not much at the studio was as he remembered it. The place was like an aircraft hanger partitioned off for businesses making jewellery, recycling electronic systems or testing robots. It was just the sort of environment an enterprise like "Live Your Dream" would slot into.

The technicians that greeted Barry were so young he felt as though he was gate crashing a student end of term party. But they were all charming, greeting him as though he was a star. There was even a medically trained attendant just in case something went wrong.

They took his coat and escorted him to a chair rather like that of his dentist's, where electrodes were applied to his balding pate. It wasn't as uncomfortable as he expected, though the weight of the goggles did tend to drag on the ears. As Barry drank the tea with the mild stimulant he wondered if any of them had watched The Maltese Falcon all the way through. Barry knew better than to enthuse about the performances of Sidney Greenstreet, Lauren Bacall, Peter Lorre and, of course, Humphrey Bogart. He didn't want to embarrass the young people by eulogising over a period they could not comprehend, so quietly allowed himself to slip into that mono Dashiel Hammett dimension.

Initially the sensation was unsettling, but as the mild opiate took effect he relaxed and, to his delight, found that he was part of the action, speaking those hard-boiled lines to his long dead idols. Barry was even allowed to face down Sidney Greenstreet and flirt with Lauren Bacall while Peter Lorre lurked sinisterly in the background, unperturbed by this newcomer and diversion from the script. It was so real, Barry wondered how long he could exist in this dream state before being snapped back to the world of his basement flat and bus pass.

So he made the most of it, continuing to talk, walk, duck bullets, and add alternative dialogue to the classic film. He became such a part of it, the fact he was sitting in a chair with electrodes stuck to his head and goggles over his eyes totally escaped him.

And then the impossible happened.

The director called 'cut!'

This was not one of the "Live Your Dream's"

technicians announcing that his time was up, but a much older voice husky with smoking and screaming directions at actors and film crew.

Barry's imaginary world had become tangible. He could feel the heat of spotlights and hear a camera cease to whirr. He was no longer in a film, but on a sound stage.

A host of attendants bustled on set to tend to their particular star, offer refreshments, or add touches to make-up. And most gratifyingly, Barry was brought a cup of tea by a beautiful young man wearing a huge silk tie. This vision in monochrome held up a mirror for the actor to check that he was still camera perfect.

This was too glorious to be real. Vigour and pain-free movement flowed through Barry's arthritic limbs and the gnarled hands that had been freckled with age spots were now powerful and wore diamond rings. Reflected in the mirror were firm features, suave with a hint of moustache. Barry was in his early thirties, glamorous as only a Hollywood star could be. All right, he may have still been in monochrome, but that was a small price to pay to live the dream fate had stolen from him.

He was a star. The young "Live Your Dream" technicians surrounding him no longer existed. Barry was determined to stay in this world they had created for him and nothing - but nothing - would drag him back to mundane reality.

All attempts to coax the customer back to reality were futile. The medical assistant had to accept that this one had been seduced by the allure of his personalised never-never land and was refusing to leave. The only indication that his brain was still functioning after the electrodes and goggles had been removed was a blissful, distant smile. Barry did manage to get up, and even speak a few words of gratitude, but he was no longer with them.

The insurance from the "Live Your Dream" policy guaranteed him that place in the home for retired actors, which happily accepted him as a harmless, easy-to-manage resident.

In his armchair in the corner of the lounge, Barry lived on in his Hollywood mansion with that beautiful young man as a companion and an entourage to pander to his every whim. His fixed, distant smile belied the fact that he was actually enjoying the fast life with visits to nightclubs and illicit gambling dens; an existence full of romance, scandal, and stardust. Barry appeared on the covers of film magazines, arm in arm with (female) models the studio obligingly supplied on a regular basis to conceal his true preferences. And of course, he drove a fast car along Sunset Boulevard and down to Rio, a flash of silver as he speeded along the Californian coast road.

Then it crashed.

The mangled wreckage must have filled newspaper front pages - but Barry no longer had any way of telling.

For a brief moment he was aware of lying on comfortable, cotton sheets, sunlight streaming through an open window as he surrendered his last gasp to the serene NHS nurse looking down at him.

The dream was over, though glorious while it lasted.

Breath of Nature

Unlike her mother, Elvira did not possess green fingers. As soon as she tried to nurture a plant into bloom, it promptly took exception, wilted and died. Retirement had given her all the time in the world to try and remedy this. As she particularly loved flowers, many more plants suffered a similar fate before it had to be accepted that horticulture, on any level, was not her forte.

There was always the Internet to fill the time, but its pop-up pages, spurious links to sites that either wanted to sell you something or infect your operating system were beginning to make it too tedious to bother with. And Facebook was a different dimension for someone who had known others so intimately as a nurse.

Then one day Elvira typed in "crocheted flowers". She didn't know why, only that she was good at was crocheting, and had often wished she could so easily crochet people back together when all medical help had failed. Why not crochet flowers instead? The members of the social club she attended regarded artificial flowers as hideous anomalies and spent much of the time bragging about their immaculate gardens filled with exotic blooms. They were all retired as well, and had the time and money to spend hours wandering the aisles of garden centres looking for that one plant which would out bloom everyone else's.

Existence to Elvira, after a career of others depending on her - often for their lives - meant much more than that, and enforced retirement was eroding the sense of what she had achieved. Now there was all the time in the world to ponder on mortality, it began to make less and less sense. So she would crochet flowers instead of trying to fill the house with living blooms. It would take her mind off all those humdrum inconsequentialities and might even help her to solve that great imponderable she had seen so many have to face - the very nature of existence.

Elvira sat in front of the computer screen, tapping away in searches for crocheted flowers, hardly expecting to find a page on how to crochet a potted plant. The best result was a website with a range of realistic looking flowers worked in fine silk and stiffened to form everything from exotic lilies, orchids - even a strelitzia - to ripe fruit. This remarkable filigree work was in one ply thread, the stitches so small they were barely visible. It was hardly surprising that the lacy petals needed to be stiffened.

The patterns and instructions on how to create them were free to download as a PDF, yet there was nothing in the covering text to suggest where the website, "Breathe of Nature", originated from.

The only problem was, did Elvira have a crochet hook that fine? Probably not. But "Breath of Nature" had an eBay account from which hooks, silk and stiffening medium could be purchased, and at a price her pension could afford. There was also a link to another website in an incomprehensible dialect. Working in the NHS and having to help patients fill in forms, Elvira was familiar with the way most languages looked. But this one could have been ancient Sumerian for all she could tell. And the flower people depicted in it were just as peculiar. It was difficult to tell if they were flowers turning into humans, or humans turning into flowers. It was all very strange, yet had a sinister parallel with her opinion of Homo sapiens, which had hardened considerably over the years. It had eventually reached the point where Elvira wondered if most people deserved to be helped. After one husband walking out because of her unsocial working hours, and the other because he had found a younger model - a trainee nurse with startlingly large eyes, despite which she still managed to administer wrong doses - there was every right to feel cynical. Or was she just getting old, and all the niggles that had built up during her lifetime reaching the point where she wished people would turn into plants?

Why not crochet flowers, free from the demands of selfish humanity, or even be transformed into a flower? Elvira wondered what that would be like.

She printed out the instruction pages then went back to the eBay listing, determined to crochet at least one bloom convincing enough to fool the neighbours when it was put in the front window.

As soon as the needles and thread arrived there were no more visits to the social club. Elvira sat for hour upon hour, happily working away at her filigree creations. Friends occasionally called to make sure that she was all right, and neighbours noticed that her groceries were now delivered. Even her cat, which used to be the centre of attention, spent most of its time basking on the front porch.

Months went by: nurses at the hospital where she used to work continued to call round every now and then, wondering why they had lost contact. Persuaded that Elvira was content and healthy enough, they left her to her consuming passion, now and then dropping in to marvel at the floral wonderland being created.

Months blurred into years and still Elvira crocheted away. Beautiful exotic pot plants appeared in every window; so many they blocked out the light. Resenting that it was no longer the centre of attention, the cat wandered off and found another home several streets away. The visits of well-meaning friends became fewer, and the members of the social club began to wonder if she was still alive.

Then one day her doctor, not having heard from Elvira for so long, and concerned that none of her prescriptions had been renewed, tried to reach her by phone. There was no reply, so Dr Kemble decided to pay her patient a visit.

Unable to raise anyone at the front door, and being a fit young woman, she climbed onto the wheelie bin and reached over to unlock the side gate. The garden had run wild, invading the side passage and making it difficult to get to the back door. Dr Kemble tried to peer through the kitchen window but flowers blocked the view. Foliage had pushed up the latch so she opened it, sending several plants tumbling into the sink.

Now she could see inside.

All the kitchen units were covered in blossoming vines, their tendrils clinging to the light fittings and plate racks. In the hallway a tangle of foliage weighed down by fruit tumbled through the banisters, using the hatstand for support. Even if the doctor could find the key, it was unlikely the rampant vegetation would have allowed the door to be pushed open. So, expecting Elvira to be lying comatose somewhere in this jungle, she clambered through the kitchen window.

Phoning for an ambulance would have been pointless before she found her patient, though a fire brigade axe might have come in useful. Pulling the vines, stems and tendrils aside, Dr Kemble forced her way through the hall, only to find that all the rooms, as well as the stairs and stairwell, were filled with the extraordinary foliage. None of the plants had roots, feeling silky and organic to the touch. As well as hanging from the light sockets, they dangled from cracks in the ceilings as though feeding on air.

After pushing huge orchids aside it was possible to see into the front room. This was full of bizarre fruit enclosing the furniture in a multi-coloured blanket.

But there was no Elvira.

Dr Kemble fought her way through the foliage and up the stairs. Only the bathroom was relatively free of plants, though there was not much evidence of it being used recently.

Things looked bad.

Yet again, the bedrooms were filled with leaves and flowers, but no Elvira. The only other place was the roof void, and it was unlikely her barely mobile patient would be up there.

Double checking the house and small overgrown garden to make sure that Elvira had totally disappeared, Dr Kemble phoned the police.

Their initial enquiries confirmed that no one had seen the retired nurse leave the house, even to visit the local supermarket, post office or chemist. The neighbours assumed Elvira to still be crocheting away with the skeins of fine silk thread that had been regularly delivered.

A forensic team was called in to do a fingertip search. It took days for them to gather up all the invasive foliage and bag it for examination. The only DNA they expected to find was that of silk worms.

Then, as it seemed suspiciously organic, they took samples from the tamarind shaped fruits the doctor had found in the front room.

Each one contained Elvira's DNA.

Callaloo

At first only Edna saw her - the phantom woman with a mug in one hand and hatchet in the other.

The other allotment holders believed that she had been hallucinating through lack of sleep. She was always getting up too early in the morning to check on her precious sweet peas and lettuces in the hope of catching the culprits that had been attacking them.

But then Bob and Daphne saw the same woman one evening while watering the runner beans, which had cropped so well that year they had been determined to grow extra for the freezer. None of the other allotment holders had been about. Most of them were either in the pub or at home in front of the TV with their cocoa. Some of them were older than the allotments which had been allocated by the local authority over 70 years ago and, apart from two latter day hippies in their early 20s, Bob and Daphne were the youngest. They knew they hadn't been hallucinating when this ghostly figure made her way through Newton's plot filled with callaloo. She was heading towards the second-hand garden shed he had recently put up to accommodate his tools and battered old armchair. As they weren't cabbage lovers, Bob and Daphne had been tempted to grow callaloo as well, but it would have taken up the room needed for their onions, courgettes, soft fruit and - most of all - runner beans.

As soon as Newton had purchased his shed on eBay, collected it in his battered old truck and assembled it with the help of several other allotment holders, he began to have misgivings about the purchase. He had never been able to say why, but felt that there was something sinister about it. Everyone dismissed this as another of his empathetic foibles. Newton used pine cones to forecast the weather, predict the future by watching the clouds, and drank redbush mixed with rum through a straw. And he was still pretty sharp for his age, never known to hallucinate.

Bob and Daphne decided not to mention the ghostly woman with a hatchet until somebody else saw the apparition.

The next evening was the allotment's monthly get-together around Norman's barbecue when everybody brought the pick of their root vegetables, courgettes and maize to be roasted.

This time the phantom's appearance couldn't even be put down to alcohol as most of them had to drive home.

Edna was the first to be aware of her presence. Then everyone else saw her, mug in one hand and hatchet in the other.

Norman was turning the parsnips and corn on the cob. He dropped the tongs into the barbecue embers with a clatter that sent up a shower of sparks.

The phantom moved purposefully, coming closer.

Everyone backed away.

Edna would have fainted, but the others were so fixated on the apparition there was no one to catch her.

There was a collective gasp of relief as the woman with the hatchet veered off towards Newton's shed.

Newton automatically followed her despite warnings from the others who chased after him at a safe distance.

This time the phantom entered his shed as though encouraged to put on a show now there was an audience. But there would be no awards for this performance. The onlookers watched in horror as she sent the hatchet crashing down onto the shadow of a man inside. Then they both faded from sight.

Eventually Newton broke the silence. 'Used to be a worktop there. I didn't put it back. I needed more space.'

'Yeah, I remember,' said Norman automatically. 'Good kindling, that was.'

Esmeralda, the hippie's, observation was more to the point. 'Who do you think she was attacking?'

That had crossed everyone else's mind, though no one else wanted to think about it - apart from Bob.

'Yes, she was definitely chopping someone up.'

Newton felt his knees buckle. 'Oh god ... I need a stiff drink.'

Norman lent a supporting arm. 'Come and have a swig of my peach brandy. I'll make sure you get home all right.'

The allotment holders lost any appetite for the vegetables now smouldering on the barbecue, and the next day there was a meeting of the allotment committee. They decided that Newton's shed had to go. It was agreed that everyone should chip in and buy him a replacement so the old one could be put on one of Norman's bonfires. But Bob and Daphne wanted to return it to the seller's address: that was the only hope they had of discovering who the phantom with the hatchet might have been. It was then that Newton confessed to discovering an old diary in the false bottom of the workbench draw that Norman had burnt.

The pages were handwritten and sometimes illegible. What could be read revealed that the writer had an obsession about being slowly poisoned. His doctor had insisted that he was imagining it all, pointing out that his wife was a generous, devoted woman unlikely to be spiking his meals with anything toxic. Why on earth would she do something like that when they had four children and another on the way? The family depended on his income and were unlikely to kill him, if only for that reason. So he apparently gave up and persuaded himself that he had been imagining it all.

The allotment committee agreed that the only way to get to the bottom of the matter was with a diplomatic visit to the seller by Newton, accompanied by Bob and Daphne, though they remained adamant that the haunted shed had to go on the bonfire.

The Cleminsons owned a smallholding on the outskirts of a neighbouring village. They had originally intended to burn the shed with all the other unused fixtures and fittings being cleared from the outhouses, but it belonged to their father and they couldn't face the thought of it not being put to some use.

When he arrived, Laura Cleminson recognised Newton immediately and invited him, Bob and Daphne in without question. She assumed their visit had something to do with a refund of the £30 he had paid for the shed, which she would have happily handed over had there been any problems.

Bob assured her that they had only come to see if there was any other garden equipment he could give a home to on his allotment.

Laura showed them to the outhouse where the old implements were stored. They had been in the family for ages, but were not old enough to offer to a museum. None of her brothers had been interested in carrying on the market garden. They had settled jobs in offices and were happy to hand it over to their youngest sister, Laura, who was building up her nursery of herbs.

Bob and Daphne discovered several free standing metal frames for climbing plants, ideal in their quest for the perfect runner bean, and paid Laura £20 for them.

Over mugs of tea, the young woman explained that life had been hard, even before their father left without warning. So her hard-working mother brought up the children to understand that everything came with a price. While the sons chose university, Laura followed in her mother's footsteps, transforming the market garden into a nursery supplying herbs and exotic vegetables to restaurants. She was enthusiastic about Newton's crop of callaloo. Before long they were sharing growing tips and the real reason for the visit no longer seem that important. Learning that Laura's father had mysteriously disappeared was enough. There would have been no point in telling the woman that they had seen the ghost of her mother wielding a hatchet inside the old shed she had lovingly disposed of.

Then, without warning, Newton's empathic genie persuaded him to lay his hand on the back of Laura's. 'Your father didn't run out on you and your brothers, you know. He really loved you and had every intention of coming back. But something happened to prevent him - you know that, don't you?'

Laura looked at him in surprise for a moment, and then smiled. 'I'm sure that's what happened. Mother always insisted that he was useless and she shouldn't have married him, but we believed that was her way of dealing with his disappearance. She wouldn't go to the police to report him missing for some reason. We assumed it was because he had become involved in something she didn't want them to know about. After she died we tried to find out more, but there was no paper trail or records to follow. It was as though he had never existed. We knew we would never find out what happened to him, so gave up trying.'

'That's the best way,' Newton reassured her. 'Sometimes you have to accept that there are things you will never know. It happens to all of us.'

Laura nodded gratefully for having someone understand a conundrum that had haunted her for years.

'I'm afraid Newton's shed has woodworm,' Daphne announced without warning. 'He wasn't going to tell you, but we will need to burn it before it infects everything else in the allotments.'

'That's all right,' said Laura, 'We had the feeling that something about it wasn't right. We should have checked more thoroughly. 'I'm sorry you went to all the bother of re-erecting it only to find that out. The most I can do is refund the money.'

She added £10 to Bob and Daphne's £20 and

offered it to Newton.

He refused to accept the money. 'No girl, you keep it. But I would like to take away a couple of your herbs.'

'You sure?'

'I'm quite sure.'

'Come into the nursery and look around. You won't believe the range we've built up. The land here is still very fertile, and we've managed to bring on varieties that have failed in other nurseries. In fact, the only plot we can't seem to grow anything on is down by the old duck pond. So we've just left it to the nettles and the butterflies; a sort of wildlife haven where the hedgehogs can make their nests. Odd that, wild flowers love the place, but plant anything else there and it just withers away.'

Printed in Great Britain
by Amazon